THIS WALKER BOOK BELONGS TO:

For Winifred Clarke
with thanks

M.M.

First published 1992
by Walker Books Ltd, 87 Vauxhall Walk
London SE11 5HJ

This edition published 1994

2 4 6 8 10 9 7 5 3 1

Text © 1992 Michelle Magorian
Illustrations © 1992 Jan Ormerod

This book has been set in ITC Garamond.

Printed in Hong Kong

British Library Cataloguing in Publication Data
A catalogue record for this book is
available from the British Library.

ISBN 0-7445-2073-8

JUMP!

Written by Michelle Magorian

Illustrated by Jan Ormerod

WALKER BOOKS
LONDON

Every Saturday morning, Steven sat with his father and watched his older sister, Theresa, at her ballet class. There were three boys in the class – Michael, Joe and Barry. Steven longed to join them. When the boys and girls jumped, Steven leaned forward and pretended he was jumping too. After the class he danced with Theresa all the way home.

One day, when the boys and girls were bending their knees at the barre, Steven overheard the teacher saying, "Remember, class, the deeper you can plié, the higher you will be able to jump." Steven watched even more closely. Jumping was the thing he liked doing best.

As soon as
he was
home he
practised.

In
the hall.

In the
kitchen.

By the bath.

"What are you doing, Steven?"
asked his mother.
"I'm pliéing like Theresa does in
dance classes."
"You don't want to do that," she said.
Steven was puzzled. I do, he thought.
"Mum, can I go to dance classes?"
His mother's mouth opened wide.
"Certainly not. Real boys
don't go to dance
classes."

The following Saturday, after the
class had done their bows and curtsies,
Steven walked over to where the boys
were putting on their tracksuits.

He squeezed Michael's arm, he touched
Joe's back and he gave Barry's hair a tug.
"What are you doing?" they asked.
"I'm seeing if you're real," said Steven.
"Well, we are," they said.

"They are real, Mum," he told his mother.
"You can play basketball," she said, looking
up from the television, "and that's that."
"What's basketball?"
"A game, a tough game, with a ball," she
said, and pointed at the screen. "Look."

"They're jumping!" he exclaimed.
"Yes," said his mum, "as high as they can."
"Good," said Steven. "Can I play it today?"
"We don't have a ball or a net, and you need somewhere to play it," she said.
"You'll have to grow a bit too."

"Oh," Steven sighed,
disappointed. He raced
into his and Theresa's
bedroom and pliéd and
leapt and flung his arms
as wildly as he could until
he felt better.

At the next class, when
the boys were jumping, Steven
couldn't sit still any longer.
He ran across the floor.
His father tried to pull him away.
"Let him stay," said the teacher.
"He's good."
After the jumps the teacher said,
"Show me what else you
can do, Steven."
So he did.

The children clapped.
"Would you like to be in
the show this year?" the
teacher asked.
"Will you teach me a basketball
dance?" asked Steven.
The teacher laughed.
"Well," she said, "I'll see."

On the night of the show,
Steven's mum and dad sat in the audience.
"Where's Steven?" his mum asked.
"He's here," said Steven's father.
"Where? I can't see him."

"You will. Later. It's a surprise."
The lights went down and the curtains opened.
There was a bumble-bee dance by the babies,
followed by a skating dance.
"It's Theresa's class next," whispered Dad.

They heard a referee's whistle and
music, then all the boys and girls
danced on stage in shorts and T-shirts.
The children spun and threw an
imaginary basketball at one another.
They jumped in all directions, patting
it around each other in circles.

Theresa, playing the referee,
whirled in and out through
the teams with her whistle,
until one team had won and
the dance was over.

The smallest and
happiest person
in the group leapt
the highest.
It was Steven.

The audience laughed and cheered.

Steven's mum was the only person not clapping.

She was too surprised even to speak.

"That small one with the red hair and freckles,
why, he can almost fly," said a woman in front of them.

"That's our Steven," said his father loudly.

The woman turned round.

"He can certainly jump, can't he?" she said, astonished.

Steven's mum was still watching the children bowing
on stage. Steven waved. His mother waved back.

"He'll make a fine basketball player one day," said the woman. "A fine player." "Yes, I think he will," said Steven's mum, and she smiled proudly. "He'll make a fine dancer too."

MORE WALKER PAPERBACKS
For You to Enjoy

EAT UP, GEMMA
by Sarah Hayes/Jan Ormerod

A story about the food exploits of baby Gemma, the youngest member of a Black English family.

"Great child appeal, accurately reflecting the warmth of family life." *Books for Keeps*

0-7445-1328-6   £3.99

THE FROG PRINCE
by Jan Ormerod

"Beautifully retold with illustrations that
are stunningly effective." *Practical Parenting*

0-7445-1787-7   £3.99

ONE BALLERINA TWO
by Vivian French/Jan Ormerod

Two young ballerinas, one small and one not-so-small, practise their
steps and movements – from ten pliés to one final hug!

"Jan Ormerod's skill in capturing exactly the movements and gestures
of small children is shown here to great effect... A witty and
informative picture book." *The School Librarian*

0-7445-3045-8   £3.99

WHEN WE WENT TO THE ZOO
by Jan Ormerod

"Wonderful animal pictures … the book as a whole adds up to
a great experience for a child." *Tony Bradman, Parents*

0-7445-2318-4   £4.99

**Walker Paperbacks are available from most booksellers, or by post from
Walker Books Ltd, PO Box 11, Falmouth, Cornwall TR10 9EN.**

To order, send: Title, author, ISBN number and price for each book ordered, your full name and address,
cheque or postal order for the total amount, plus postage and packing:

UK and BFPO Customers – £1.00 for first book, plus 50p for the second book and plus 30p for each additional book to a maximum charge of £3.00.
Overseas and Eire Customers – £2.00 for first book, plus £1.00 for the second book and plus 50p per copy for each additional book.
Prices are correct at time of going to press, but are subject to change without notice.